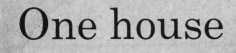

One house

TWO MICE

Sergio Ruzzier

CLARION BOOKS
Houghton Mifflin Harcourt
Boston   New York

Three cookies.

Three boats
Two oars

One rower.

One nest
Two eggs

Three ducklings.

Three rocks

Two holes

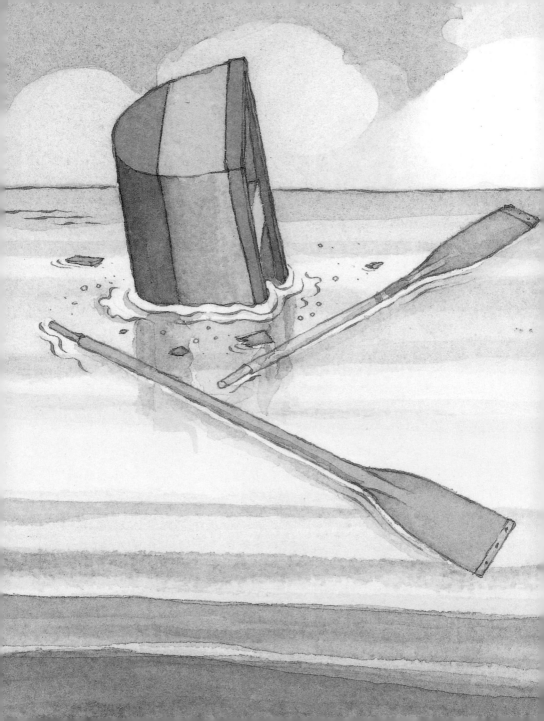

One shipwreck.

One island
Two trees

Three tears.

Three beaks

Two snacks?

One escape.

One path
Two stars

Three cheers!

Three carrots
Two onions

One soup.

To George Nicholson

Clarion Books • 215 Park Avenue South • New York, New York 10003 • Copyright © 2015 by Sergio Ruzzier
All rights reserved. For information about permission to reproduce selections from this book, write to
Permissions, Houghton Mifflin Harcourt Publishing Company, 215 Park Avenue South, New York, New York 10003.
Clarion Books is an imprint of Houghton Mifflin Harcourt Publishing Company. • www.hmhco.com
The illustrations in this book were done in pen and ink and watercolors on paper. The text was set in 32 pt. Century School Book Std.
Library of Congress Cataloging-in-Publication Data is available • ISBN 978-0-544-30209-9
Manufactured in China • SCP 10 9 8 7 6 5 4 3 2 1   4500529166